For Rebecca

Barefoot Beginners *an imprint of* Barefoot Books, 37 West 17th Street, 4th Floor East, New York, New York 10011
Text and illustrations copyright © 2000 by Caroline Mockford. The moral right of Caroline Mockford to be identified as the author and illustrator of this work has been asserted. First published in the United States of America in 2000 by Barefoot Books, Inc.
All rights reserved. No part of this book may be reproduced in any form or by any means, electronic or mechanical, including photocopying, recording, or by any information storage and retrieval system, without permission in writing from the publisher
Printed on 100% acid-free paper. This book was typeset in Gill Sans Bold 22 point on 30 point leading. The illustrations were prepared in acrylics on 140lb watercolor paper. Graphic design by Judy Linard, England. Color separation by Grafiscan, Italy.
Printed in Hong Kong / China by South China Printing Co. (1988) Ltd
1 3 5 7 9 8 6 4 2

US Cataloging-in-Publication Data
Mockford, Caroline.
    What's this? / written and illustrated by Caroline Mockford.—1st ed.
[32]p. : col. ill. ;   cm.
Summary: A small girl finds a seed and, with her friends, discovers how it grows into a beautiful sunflower. Stylish artwork and a page of helpful information about how plants grow make this an engaging gift book and valuable science resource in the classroom.
ISBN 1-84148-018-5
1. Seeds—Juvenile literature. 2. Sunflowers—Juvenile literature. I. Title.
    631.5/ 31 —dc21   1999   AC   CIP

What's This?

written and illustrated by
Caroline Mockford

BAREFOOT BOOKS

A seed lay on the ground.

One winter morning,
a bird saw the seed.

He flew down to have a closer look.

The bird hopped around the seed.
He looked at it
from the left
and he looked at it
from the right.

"What's this?" thought the bird.

A little girl came by.
She, too, looked at the seed.
"What's this?" she wondered.
"Let's find out,"
she said to
the bird.

A ginger cat came by.
The little girl planted the seed
carefully in a corner of her garden.
"What's this?" she asked the cat.
The cat looked at the girl wisely.

"It's something that grows,"
she said. "You will have to give it some
water."

**The little girl listened and remembered.
On days when it rained, she did not water
the seed, but on days when it was sunny,
she gave it a long, cool drink.**

Spring came to the garden.
The bird and the little girl and the
marmalade cat watched and waited.
The seed started to grow.
A thin stem
pushed out of the ground,
and two small leaves
opened at the top.

Soon
the plant
was
taller
than
the bird.
It grew more leaves,
and its stem
became
longer
and
longer.

Summer came to the garden. Now the plant was taller than the cat. The sun grew hotter and hotter; sometimes the little girl had to water the plant twice a day. Its stem became so long that she had to tie it to a stick to stop it from falling over.

Every day when she woke up,
the little girl ran straight out to
the garden to look at the plant
that was growing from the seed.

And one morning,
when she ran outside,
there, turning its head
to the sun, was a
magnificent sunflower.

Whenever she could, the
little girl visited the sunflower.
She told it all of her secrets.
The ginger cat and the bird
watched and listened.

Fall

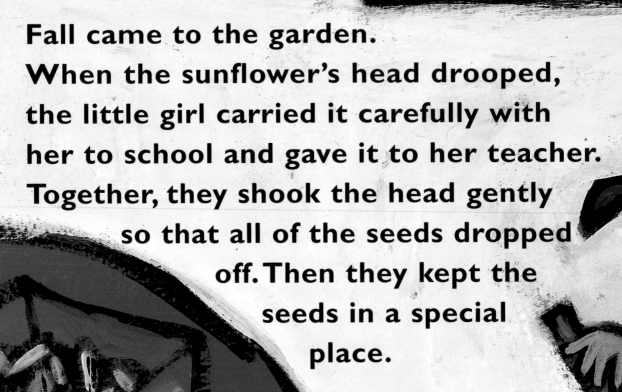

Fall came to the garden.
When the sunflower's head drooped,
the little girl carried it carefully with
her to school and gave it to her teacher.
Together, they shook the head gently
so that all of the seeds dropped
off. Then they kept the
seeds in a special
place.

Winter passed and spring returned.
The children in the class planted
their sunflower seeds in pots.

Every day they watered them
and watched them.

And when the next summer came,
every child had a beautiful,
smiling sunflower!

Roots, Shoots, Flowers, and Seeds

Many of the plants in gardens, parks and fields, and all of the vegetables that we eat, come from seeds. Seeds come in thousands of shapes and sizes. Plants grow from seeds and many of them produce flowers. Plants need food, water and sunshine to become strong and healthy, to flower and to make the seeds that produce next year's plants.

Roots

Seeds store up energy so that, when they are planted in the ground, they can grow roots downward into the soil. The roots suck up water and food from the earth. This gives the plant the energy to grow shoots. If you plant a broad bean in a clear plastic cup, you will be able to watch the roots growing down into the earth and the shoots growing upward.

Shoots

Most plants grow in spring and summer, when the sun gets hotter and warms the earth. Green shoots push upward through the soil toward the sun, until you can see them growing above ground. Leaf buds at the tip of the shoot uncurl into tiny leaves. The leaves of the plant catch the sunlight and turn it into more food, until the plant has enough energy to make flowers.

Flowers

Flowers make nectar, a sweet, sugary liquid, which bees collect to make honey. As the bees suck up nectar from the flowers, a bright yellow powder ("pollen"), brushes onto them. When they fly into the next flower, the pollen brushes off them again. This "pollinates" the flower, so that new seeds begin to grow in the flower head.

Seeds

When the flower head dies, the seeds fall to the ground or are carried off by insects, birds or the wind and dropped far away. The seeds work their way into the soil during the fall and, the following year, more plants grow from them.

Growing Sunflowers

Sunflowers can grow from a tiny seed into a plant up to 15ft high!
When you have grown a sunflower and collected the seeds from the drooping flower head, you can share them with your friends and plant them in the spring. If there is room in your garden, you can make a secret sunflower den by planting the seeds in a rectangle (leave space for a door). When the plants grow tall, you will have your own summer house!

BAREFOOT BOOKS publishes high-quality picture books for children of all ages and specializes in the work of artists and writers from many cultures. If you have enjoyed this book and would like to receive a copy of our current catalog, please contact our New York office — Barefoot Books Inc., 37 West 17th Street, 4th Floor East, New York, New York 10011

e-mail: ussales@barefoot-books.com

website: www.barefoot-books.com